JACK RYDER

The Long
RIDE HOME

EROTIC ROMANCE

WARNING

This book contains sexually explicit scenes and adult language. It may be considered offensive to some readers. This book is for sale to adults ONLY.

* * * * * * * * * * * * * * * * * * * *

Please store your files wisely where they cannot be accessed by underage readers.

Please feel free to send me an email. Just know that these emails are filtered by my publisher. Good news is always welcome.

Jack Ryder - **jack_ryder@awesomeauthors.org**

About the Publisher

4Fun Publishing, a member of **BLVNP Incorporated**, 340 S. Lemon #6200, Walnut CA 91789, info@blvnp.com / legal@blvnp.com
NOTE: Due to the highly emotional reaction of some people to works of erotic fiction, any email sent to the above address that contains foul language or religious references is automatically deleted by our anti-spam software and will not be seen. All other communications are welcome.

DISCLAIMER

The Long Ride Home
Erotic Romance

By: Jack Ryder

© Jack Ryder 2014
ISBN: 978-1-62761-750-5

Chapter One

When I was discharged from the service my final posting had been in Germany. When I got back to the States, I found that the "free" shipment of my brand new BMW station wagon meant that the Government got it across the water for me, but it was up to me to get it from Charleston, South Carolina, to my home in Seattle. I would have to drive all the way across the United States with the threat of winter approaching.

To add to my joy, I found that my vehicle was nearly out of fuel. This, despite the fact I had filled it up just before turning it in for shipment. I was not a happy traveller when I pulled in to the truck stop fuel station just off the expressway on the edge of town. It was just getting dark on that third Friday in November. I could see the steam of my breath as I got out to fuel the car.

I was thinking to myself that I had better get a room and just start the drive home in the morning. Early! As I glanced across the street, I felt like at least one thing might work out OK today. Directly across the expressway there was a seedy looking little motel. The sign on the window said," Vacancy." At least I would not have to drive all over an unfamiliar town just to find a bed to sleep in. Seedy or not, a bed was all I needed.

I saw her approaching me as I was putting the fuel nozzle back in its cradle. She was a slender little thing and maybe all of 5 foot 2 inches tall. She was wearing one of those warm types of jackets with the white fur around the collar and around the wrists. Her indecently short tight hot pants were shiny black leather. The black fishnet stockings had little rips and holes in them. She was also wearing a pair of soft leather moccasin style boots that came about to mid-calf and the top 4 inches was a soft black fur. *"That's a hooker!"* I thought to myself.

"Looking for a date, Mister?" she asked quietly as she glanced around.

I was smiling since she had just confirmed my suspicions. "If I were, you would be the first in line!" I told her slyly. I had no intentions of getting laid tonight. Just a good night of sleep, then I'd be on my way home.

She looked concerned when I told her that exactly. "Look, it's supposed to snow tonight." Her voice sounded almost apologetic. "What I really need is a place to stay so I don't freeze to death out here tonight!" She told me very softly.

I stepped back to take a better look at her. She really is a pretty little thing. "I am 22!" She informed me. She must have seen me wondering if she was underage. "Most guys like to pretend that I'm much younger than that!" She sort of hesitated to divulge that. There was a slight sadness in her voice.

I could see that she was shivering as the after dusk breeze had a foreboding chill to it. "I can get the room half price for you!" She whispered her offer. When I did not answer her immediately, she smiled at me sweetly. "For thirty bucks, we could both spend the night!" She stepped forward and wrapped her arm in mine. "Pleeeeeze... I promise to make it worth your trouble!" She batted her pretty amber brown eyes at me as she said it.

As I glanced down at her, I could see straight down her jacket. I got a good look at those creamy white little tits. "OK. But just for tonight!" I whispered it. "Tomorrow I'm going home to Seattle!" I said it mostly to remind myself what the priority is. She jumped into my arms and hugged me tightly.

"My name is Nicki, by the way," she giggled as she stepped back. "I promise I'll be especially good for you!" she said it as I was letting her in the passenger door. As she bent forward, I got a very good look at her perky tits since her jacket was unzipped half way down. *"I hope I won't regret this!"* I thought to myself. She pulled her jacket all the way open as I got into the driver side. "They are yours for the night, sweetie!" She told me as I started the car.

NICKI SUGGESTED that I wait outside while she got us the room. I must admit that I felt a little giddy as I watched her walk into that office. After fifteen minutes had passed, I had begun to think that she had run off with the two twenties I had given her for the room. *"Great. Now I'll have to pay twice as much for that damn room!"* I chastised myself as I approached the office door.

I was stunned when I saw what was happening through the glass front door. I could see the clerk leaning back against the wall. His head was tilted back and his hands were on her head. Nicki was in her knees, her jacket was on the floor beside her and her head was bobbing up and down on his prick. "Yes, baby. Suck it. Suck it!" I could just barely hear his grunts through the glass door. "Oooh yes, Baby. Here it is! Here it is!" I saw him thrust his hips forward as he forced his dick farther down her throat.

A few seconds later, I saw a slow ooze of white creamy spunk drool out of her mouth as he pulled his cock out and yanked up his pants. "Best head I ever had!" He laughed it as he tossed a room key onto the counter.

When Nicki stood up, I got a good long look at her gorgeous small upturned breasts before she put her jacket back on. My dick was swelling quickly as I watched her shove the room key in one pocket and the forty bucks into the other. I quickly retreated from the door as she zipped up her jacket. I was leaning against the BMW smoking a cigarette when she came outside. "Sorry, he didn't have any change!" she lied. I figured that the forty bucks was worth a room for the night and her charms. "That's OK, baby!" I answered her softly.

As soon as we were inside room 18 on the far end of the building facing the highway, Nicki removed her jacket and threw it into the stuffed chair in the corner of the room. As she turned to face me, I could feel my heart beginning to race. The white triangles on her breasts from her tan line made her tits look so deliciously sexy. She pulled off the wool cap on her head and I saw her short sandy brown hair for the first time. Her eyes were beaming as she glanced up at me.

"I like the way you look at me, Aaron!" She said it softly as she bent over to unzip the back of both her boots. She laughed when she saw the surprised look in my face since I had not told her my name. "I glanced at your license when you got the money out of your wallet." She told me as she sat on her jacket to remove her boots. "It also said Seattle Washington, 28 years old, at least according to the birth date. And you are 6 foot 2 and 190 pounds." She smiled sweetly. "And I can clearly see that you have the same amber brown eyes that I have."

My mouth was hanging open as she stood up and wiggled out of her very tight hot pants. "My God, you are pretty!" There was the sound of amazement in my voice as she kicked off her pants and stockings at the same time. She just stood there naked for several moments as I ogled every inch of her flawless nubile body. My entire body was trembling as she walked to me and kissed me on the cheek. "I want to be clean for you." She whispered it in my ear and then she nibbled on my earlobe.

She then asked me to give her some time alone in the bathroom. "Don't worry, I'll save some hot water for you!" she giggled as she grabbed her backpack with her belongings. "I just want to look my best for you," she added. As I watched her going into the bathroom, I thought to myself that she couldn't possibly be any sexier. The lily white triangles on her breasts, ass and pubic area were the most erotically sexy thing I had ever seen. My cock was fully erect by the time she closed the door behind her.

Although the water had only run for about 10 minutes after she entered the bathroom, she was in there for nearly 45 minutes. I heard the hair dryer and some rustling around but it just seemed like a long time to me. "Are you OK in there?" I called through the door. I heard her laugh softly on the other side of the door. "Step back and close your eyes!" It sounded like her voice was very close.

I placed both hands over my face after I took a couple of steps back. I heard the squeak as the door opened and I heard her step into the room. I suddenly smelled the wonderful fragrance of lilacs and then I felt the softness of her warm hands as she reached up and cupped my face in them. "I'm all yours, Aaron." I felt her kiss the side of my neck.

"Oooh Geeeezus, Nicki, look at you!" She was wearing a matching cherry red panty and bra set that was spectacular. The panties were called a "Cheeky Thong". The front appeared like any other type of thong with the small patch covering her pussy. But the back had a little more fabric that sort of embellished the roundness of the ass cheeks. The bra was one of those fancy push up bras that adds two cup sizes and creates more cleavage. With her short boy style haircut, she looked sexy beyond belief. "You are so beautiful!" I gasped softly.

As I reached to pull her closer, she slapped my hand. "Shower first!" she laughed playfully. I gave her a playful "pouty lip" look and she laughed out loud. "You can pout all you want but it you want some of this," she pulled down her panties to show her bare pussy, "then you better clean that." She reached out and patted my swelling pecker.

As I closed the bathroom door, I decided to turn the tables on her a bit. I would take my sweet ass time getting ready too. I could hear soft music coming from the other room as I shaved my face. Then I trimmed my goatee and my eyebrows. In the shower, I washed everywhere very thoroughly and used conditioner in my hair and on my goatee. I intended to spend some quality time with my face between her legs. I sort of giggled to myself with that thought.

"You can keep the change!" I froze in the doorway as I saw her standing at the front door in those sexy underwear paying the pizza boy. His eyes were wide as saucers and I swear he was drooling. He had a huge bulge in his jeans. "Oh you should do something about that!" she reached out and patted his boner. His face was beet red as she closed the door.

I could feel my cock struggling to press out of the towel I had around my waist. "We are going to eat first!" she announced cheerfully as she set the pizza on the dresser. My head dropped and I slowly wiggled it back and forth. "Whatever you want, sweetie," I whispered my capitulation. I have to admit that her wonderful giggle made my heart melt. "Now you get it!" she laughed. I practically wolfed down the two slices of pizza. Then I gargled with mouthwash to be nice and fresh for her.

I was surprised how antsy I felt as she went in the bathroom to freshen back up. I had only known this girl less than two hours and yet, I felt a desperate need to please her. I wanted to be the best sex partner she had ever been with. But that was unlikely, considering her profession. I felt my dick swelling rapidly as I looked at her lovely butt cheeks bent over the bathroom sink. I felt the insatiable urge to go in there, rip her panties down and bury my face between those perfectly round little cheeks. I was fully erect as she finally turned off the sink water and turned to come back to me.

My dick was so rigid that it was bouncing against my stomach with the knob just under my belly button. "Oooh my, is that for me?" She said it in a playful tone as she gawked at my 9-inch prick. "Oh yes, baby, every particle is for you!" I answered her happily. She slid onto the bed next to me and leaned over to kiss me passionately. As our tongues darted in and out each other's mouth, I felt her soft warm hand wrap around my manhood. "Oh God," I gasped into her mouth.

It's funny how things never go as you had imagined. When she was bent over the sink, it had been my intention to throw her on her back, rip her panties off and then fuck her very savagely as she writhed beneath me. When she slid down and took my pounding cock into her mouth, that all evaporated. "Oooh yes, Nicki. Anything you want, baby, anything you want," I purred with delight. The sensation of her hot slobbering mouth on my prick was electrifying. I reached down and ran my fingers through her very short soft hair as she very slowly sucked my cock for me. I was like putty in her hands now. I would gladly do anything she wanted. "Sooooo good, Baby. So good!" The sound of my voice was filled with pleasure and lust.

Nicki slowly had her way with me for like this for nearly twenty minutes. She brought me just to the edge of climax about a half dozen times and then squeezed cruelly on the head of my dick to make the sensation go away and stop me from ejaculating. By the end of this time, my entire body felt like a live wire with a thousand volts of electricity coursing through me. My balls were stinging and felt like they would explode at any second. "Fuck me, Nicki. Please fuck me now!" I screamed in exquisite agony.

Nicki lifted her face from my dick and just giggled at me. "Only if you make me a promise!" She said it very softly as she continued to very slowly stroke my dick with her hand. Keeping right at the edge of bliss. "Anything! Anything!" I screamed it at her. Nicki bent forward and licked up a long strand of precum that was oozing from my hole, flicking her tongue around the head just enough to renew the electrical charge stinging my testicles. "Take me to Seattle with you, Aaron. Take me all the way!"

"Oh God yes. Anything, anything," I screamed. I felt her hot lips engulfing my prick till my whole 9 inches were buried in her throat. "Oh geeezus...geeeeeeeezus!" My legs were vibrating in spasms now. As I felt the electricity radiating in my nuts, she slowly slid her hand up behind me and started rubbing on my ass pucker "Ooooh Nicki. Ooooh Nicki," I did not recognise the deep guttural voice that was coming from my own mouth.

Just as I felt the load about to erupt, Nicki shoved her middle finger all the way up my ass. "Ooooh fuuuuuuuuuck yesssss...fuuuuuuck yesssss!" My cock exploded into her mouth with such force that it gagged her and my cum gushed out of her mouth onto my thighs. She continued to wiggle her finger inside my rectum as another spasm blasted into her throat and then another. As she slowly pulled her finger out of my ass, I shot off one last time.

My entire body was bouncing on the bed like Linda Blair in the Exorcist, as she bent forward and licked the last bit of the cream off the knob of my prick. Then she bent farther and licked up all of the cum on my thighs. "I will hold you to that!" she giggled as she wiped her mouth with the back of her hand. She scooted up and kissed me with her cum smeared lips. "But I will make you very happy that you brought me along!" She nibbled on my earlobe as she said it.

Although I was disappointed that I had not got to fuck her yet, I was amazed beyond belief at how completely this woman had satisfied me. No woman had ever given me this type of intense pleasure. No one had ever brought me to the edge so many times and then rocked my entire foundation free of all its senses. Nicki crawled up next to me and rested her head on my shoulder as she gently petted my chest with her fingers.

"I'm not a whore, Aaron. I'm not a whore." She whispered it so softly that I could barely hear the words. Over the next 20 minutes while we laid together resting, Nicki told me that she is really a model. She works for a famous lingerie company and had come to South Carolina on an offer by a movie producer to make her a TV star. After he had taken sexual liberties with her for over a week, he had kicked her out of his limo and told her to find her own way home.

Chapter Two

Nicki had tears in her eyes as she told me the rest of her story. "He told me a whore like me should be able to get back to Seattle within a matter of days!" After sobbing a bit, she told me that she has been trying for ten days to get enough money together to get a bus ticket home. She informed me that her agency had no idea that she had come out here to audition for a TV show and could fire her if they found out. Then she told me that she had a photo shoot that is scheduled for the Monday after Thanksgiving. "As long as I get there on time, things should be OK!" She informed me.

I was feeling really shitty now. I had just used her like all of those other smarmy men. I made her suck me off for a promise to give her a ride with every intention of dumping her at the first chance. "I'm so sorry!" I whispered it to her. "I'm just as horrendous..." she placed a finger over my lips to silence me.

"You are my knight in shining armour, Aaron. You are going to take me home!" She nuzzled her head into my chest and kissed me gently. "And I'll be your damsel in sexy panties!" she teased me playfully.

We fell to sleep like that with her draped over me with her head on my shoulder. I awoke about 3 a.m. because her body heat had left the bed. I watched her with my eyes mostly closed so she did not know I was watching her. I saw her eyes open wide when she found the envelope in my jacket pocket. In that envelope is two thousand dollars in traveler's checks that I have not signed. It would be effortless for her to cash them, get an airline ticket and be home in Seattle by early this afternoon.

I did not say a word as I watched her quietly get some clothes out of her bag and sneak into the bathroom to get dressed. As I waited for her to come back out, I reasoned to myself that this poor woman has been subjected to more cruelty and self-centered lust than anyone should ever have to live with. I made a decision to just let her go. I could replace the money in the morning when the nearest bank opens up.

Nicki had been in the bathroom for quite some time. I thought that I heard some muffled sobs but with the door closed, it was too muffled to be certain. When Nicki came back out, she was wearing only her cherry red cheeky panties. She had removed her bra and she just set it down with the rest of her clothes on the floor by her bag. I watched in disbelief as she quietly put the envelope back where she had found it.

She was trembling when she crawled back into the bed and scooted her body up against mine. I felt her kiss the back of my neck very gently. Several minutes later, her breathing became very soft as she dozed off to sleep. I was amazed! I think it was that exact moment that I decided that I had to keep this woman in my life somehow. Not because she was a famous and sexy model, or great in bed. Only because she is wonderful. I fell asleep soon after.

Since I had not set an alarm, it was well after daybreak when I woke up. I may have slept even later, but Nicki had other plans. I felt her kissing the back of my neck as I slowly became awake. The feeling of her warm perky breasts mashed against my back was delicious to me. But not nearly as yummy as her soft hand gently fondling my swelling prick. "You owe me a good fuck," she whispered in my ear. Then she gently bit on my earlobe. "I am going to fuck you all the way to Seattle!" Her hand had worked my cock into a throbbing frenzy already.

"You don't have to..." She reached up and put her hand over my mouth before I could finish telling her that she didn't have to fuck me for a ride to Seattle.

"If you don't roll over and fuck me right now, I will tie you to the bed and take it myself!" she growled in my ear. I felt a sudden ooze of seminal fluid as it registered that she wanted me! "Your damsel wants you in her sexy panties!" she whispered as she rubbed her thumb back and forth across the head of my prick lubricated by the oozing precum.

As I rolled onto my back, she slid on top and straddled my lap. Once again, my intent to nail her to the bed was thwarted as she grabbed my prick and guided it straight into her drenched sex hole. She hadn't even taken her panties off. She had just yanked them to the side and mounted my rigidness. "Ooooh god you feel good!" she gasped. Her body shivered a bit as my 9-inch dick bottomed out in her hungry cunt.

Nicki very slowly ground herself back and forth on my prick for several minutes as if she was memorizing every moment and every thrust. The look on her face was the most wonderful expression of greedy desire I had ever seen. The little sounds that were escaping her mouth were not quite grunts and not quite a moan. It was more like an unintentional verbal quiver. It was turning me on so much that my dick was pounding with every heartbeat as she humped me and vibrated.

Just as she was leaning back, I rolled us over, pinning Nicki on her back. "Oooh fuck yes." Her moan was a very deep husky gasp as I shoved my dick all the way in till my balls were mashed against her. As I slowly pulled back out, I raised up with my arms so I could watch my dick slipping out of her greedy hole. Her pussy lips gripped my cock so tightly that I watched with amazement as they stretched out holding on to the very last moment and then moving back in as I pressed forward.

I did this a couple more times until I was so filled with lust that I just had to start pounding into her with abandon. Smack, smack, smack, smack. My belly pounded against hers as I finally got to fuck her as savagely as my rampant lust had wanted so desperately. "Fuck me...Fuck me...Fuck me," her cries of pleasure came out as grunted gasps. Her arousal was making her pussy so wet that it was making squishy noises as I humped into her over and over. As I glanced at her lovely body with the white triangles on her tits and pussy I was overwhelmed by her tremendous sexiness.

"Oooh, Nicki. Ooooh, Nicki. Yessssssss!" As my cock began to ejaculate deep into her saucy vagina, it was the most wonderful sensation I had ever felt. Rather than several powerful spasms, the cum just flowed out of my dick in one very long continuous stream as my body convulsed uncontrollably. The heat of my sticky seed flooding into her womb sent Nicki over the edge and her body convulsed too as she exploded into her orgasm. We kissed and petted each other for a very long while afterward.

While we frolicked in the shower afterward, Nicki admitted to me that she had nearly ran off with my money in the middle of the night. "It's Ok, baby. I left it there for you!" I whispered it in her ear softly. "I couldn't stand the thought of anyone using you again, not even me!" There were tears in her eyes when she spun into my arms and kissed me so passionately that I almost thought that my lungs would collapse. "You are my knight in armour!" she murmured into my ear.

I felt like I was floating on air as we got ready to leave for Seattle. Nicki had told me that this had been the best night in her entire life. In my heart, I felt the same way. It was a surprise to me that someone so lovely would even take interest in someone as average as me. I felt like it was some sort of cosmic mistake that had accidently thrown us together like this. But at this instant, I was very thankful for the cosmic boo boo. I was now looking forward to this three thousand-mile drive. The estimated 45 hours of driving now seemed much less daunting for me.

We had been on the expressway about ten minutes when Nicki asked me if I had a cell phone charger. She explained to me that her cell phone has been dead for the last eight days because she had not brought a charger with her when she came to Carolina. I told her there was a car plug in charger in the glove box. Almost immediately after she plugged it in, she began getting an endless series of ring tones for texts and missed phone calls. She quickly turned the phone to off, allowing it to charge in silence.

As I continued on up the expressway, I noticed that Nicki had become very quiet. She had not uttered a single word in over 20 minutes.

She had not even as much as glanced my way. It seemed like she was completely off somewhere else. "Is everything OK, baby?" I finally broke the silence. The look on her face looked like dread as she turned herself to face me. She just sat there looking at me for several moments like she had no idea what to say. "Are you Ok?" I repeated it softly. I could see that her face looked white as a ghost as her eyes met mine.

"I'm married, Aaron." I could not believe I had heard those words come out of her mouth. "I know I should have told you before."

My heart was in my throat and my head felt like it was going to explode. "Before what?" I screamed it. "Before you sucked me off like a whore? Before you blackmailed a ride out of me? Before you made my heart....?" I bit my tongue before I told her I had fallen for her. I could at least save myself that small amount of dignity.

Nicki had opened her mouth as if she wanted to say something but thought the better of it and turned to face forward. There were tears rolling down her face for several minutes but she remained silent. "Don't worry, I'll take you to Seattle!" I growled at her. "A promise is a promise in my book!" When she reached over to touch my leg, I pushed her hand away. I then stuck my Bluetooth in my right ear and turned on the MP3 player. "Heavy metal, continuous!" I ordered the device. Now I would not have to deal with her sniffling or attempts at conversation.

We remained silent for the next four hours. Just after we passed the border into eastern Tennessee, she tapped me on the elbow and asked if we could stop to use the toilet. I decided this would be a good time to fill up with gas. While we were there, I heard Nicki screaming into her cell phone. "You son-of-a-bitch. You set this up! You let that pervert use me like this!" There was a lot of swearing and name calling that followed. "I hope you burn in hell, motherfucker!" She screamed it and then hung up.

She was still sobbing when I returned to the car. Even as pissed off as I have been over the last four hours, it was difficult to not feel bad for her. The lost look of despondency was clearly visible on her face. She looked like she felt completely betrayed and abandoned. My heart felt broken for her. I reached over and set my hand on her knee. "I'm sorry, Nicki!" I whispered it. I could feel her trembling as I let my hand just rest there gently. "I'd be willing to listen if you need to talk about it."

Nicki seemed a little calmer as I took my hand back and turned the key in the ignition. She leaned over and placed her head on my shoulder as I pulled out onto the expressway. She fell asleep with her head on my shoulder and the car was silent as I made my way west through Tennessee. I was not very happy as we approached Nashville. I had wanted to make it all the way to St. Louis today, but I was running out of steam quickly. I pulled into the first hotel I saw at the very edge of the city. I saw the disappointment in her face when I asked the clerk for a room with two beds.

We stopped and ate dinner in the hotel restaurant before going up to our room. While we were waiting for our food, I told Nicki that I was still willing to listen when she was ready to talk. She had a look of hopefulness on her face as our food was delivered to the table. "Before you start, there is something you need to understand." I said it softly. "You need to know where I am coming from," I added. Nicki told me that she was willing to listen too.

While we were eating, I told her about me. Or at least, I told her some of the things that have happened in my life in my relationships. I told her how my first wife ran off with another man during my first enlistment in the military while I was in Iraq. Then I told her how I came home half way through my second enlistment to find that wife six months pregnant when I had not been home in over nine months. I confided that I have not even tried another relationship in these last two years.

"What happened with us last night..." I paused, afraid to let her in. Afraid to admit that she had touched me so deeply. "It was unexpected!" I told her. "I found it hard to believe that someone as beautiful as you could really be interested in someone as plain and average as me!" I confided. "What happened last night was very special,"

I told her a half truth. Not wanting her to know it was the most terrific night of my life. "But I never believed for a moment that it would ever amount to anything more," I lied.

"Oooh, Aaron!" Nicki had reached over and laid her hand on my arm. But the waitress came with the meal stub before she could continue. I paid for the meal and we made it to our room. "I think it's best that we sleep in separate beds," I informed her as I dropped my suitcase next to the bed nearest the bathroom. "Until we get this sorted out." As hurt and confused as I was, my body still craved her. I wanted to throw her on the bed and fuck her till she would promise to be mine and only mine.

I told Nicki that I was exhausted and wanted to take a shower before going to bed. I told her that we could talk after I finished my shower. I didn't hear her come into the bathroom or the shower door opening up. I had just begun to rinse the shampoo from my hair when I felt a cold breeze of air against my ass. Then I felt her warm naked body press up against mine as her arms wrapped around my waist.

"You listen to me, Aaron Mylow. There is nothing plain or average about you. That's bullshit!" She said it in a sassy sort of voice. I could feel her body becoming slippery from the soapy water as she gently rubbed herself against my back. "What happened last night was special for me too!" she whispered it in my ear before she bit gently on my earlobe. "It was the most wonderful night I've ever had!" I could feel my dick swelling as she moved her hands up to pinch on my nipples.

She moved her hands back down to my waist and gave a tug so I would turn around to face her. As her gorgeous naked body came into my view, I heard an old Star Trek line pass through my brain. *"Resistance is Futile!"* I could feel myself trembling as I glanced at her golden tanned body with the sexy white triangles from her bikini tan line. "You are not the only one who has had fucked up shit happen to you!" She had a look of determination on her face. "And you are not the only one who is afraid of being hurt!" She leaned and planted a gentle kiss on my chest.

My cock was fully rigid when she reached down and grasped it gently. "This tells me that you still desire me!" she said it playfully. "And I think we should do something about that right now!" Before I could reply, she bent forward and engulfed my prick with her hot wet mouth.

"Oooh, Nicki. Oooh God. Yes!" I groaned softly.

Once she had my dick oozing precum, she hopped up and wrapped her legs around my waist. "Fuck me like you mean it!" she gasped as she guided my dick into her sexhole. "Take me, Aaron…Please take me!" She moaned it in my ear.

I turned and pressed her against the shower wall. Bam, Bam, Bam, Bam….I slammed her against the wall over and over as I pounded into her. With all the stress and pent up emotions, this only lasted less than two minutes. My legs vibrated as my seed flooded deep into her quivering pussy.

Chapter Three

Before we went to sleep together that night, in the same bed, Nicki told me the rest of her story. She told me how she had married her husband Randy just after she turned 18. She had met him at a graduation party. Although he was ten years older and not particularly good looking, he was a successful photographer with many contacts. He had promised her to make her famous.

Randy had not told her that he would expect her to sleep with the producers and other related people that could help her career to progress. She had never dreamed that his main sexual motive was to watch her being sexually exploited by others. That included the parade of other young girls that he had seduced and brought home for her to have sex with while he sat nearby and pleasured himself as he watched.

"Last night was the first time in my life that I felt truly wanted!" She had gently touched my face as she said it. "The way you look at me, the way that you touch me, the way you take me." She smiled sweetly at me and kissed me on the cheek. "You are the only man that has ever wanted just me, all of me!" I felt a little guilty now for my anger with her earlier.

"Yeah, but I am much worse than all of them. I want all of you for myself!" I answered her.

"You silly man!" she giggled joyously. "That's why I love you, Aaron. You want all of me!" Nicki had then climbed on top of me and made love to me before we finally went to sleep in one another's arms.

NICKI WAS in the shower when I woke up in the morning. I saw her cell phone on the dresser and could not contain my curiosity.

Nicki had told me that she had been coerced into performing some very disgusting sex acts and that they had been recorded. This had been arranged by her husband so he could use the recordings to blackmail her into giving him half their assets. He was about to dump her so he could marry the newest model in her agency. A cute little 18 year old red head named Amanda. He was threatening to turn the recordings over to agency which could ruin her.

There were two dozen photos that Randy had sent to her cell phone and a one-minute video of what Hank, the producer, had done to her in South Carolina. I felt sick to my stomach as I made myself watch the video. The old man had her head in his hands and he humped into her throat relentlessly as she gagged and long strands of precum and saliva gushed from her mouth. Then after he pulled out and sprayed his cum all over her face, he had made her squat in the middle of the living room and urinate for him.

There were photographs of Hank fucking her up the ass and another of him masturbating on her tits. There were several other men that she had been filmed sucking their cocks. I was able to recognise that all three of these men were photographers. Each of them was holding an expensive camera and was snapping photos of her sucking while they were being photographed in these photos by someone else. Probably Randy himself. I had just set the cell phone back on the dresser when Nicki came out of the bathroom wrapped only in a large bath towel.

My face must have been white as a ghost. I was stunned and sickened by what I had just seen. My heart felt broken for the savage depravity that she had been subjected to. I didn't even feel the tears running down my face as she slowly walked towards me. "I'm so sorry, Nicki. I'm so sorry that happened to you." My voice was trembling noticeably.

Nicki wrapped her arms around my waist and laid her head against my chest. "I don't care anymore, Aaron. I just don't care!" she whispered. "I will just give him what he wants and quit modeling too!" I could hear the determination and resolve in her voice. She lifted her head to look into my eyes. "I have everything I need as long as I still have you!" she whispered it and then kissed my cheek again gently.

Nicki let her towel drop to the floor as she stepped back from me. "I hope what you saw didn't change how you feel about me!"

As I gawked at her gorgeous naked body and considered all I had learned about her, it made me even more incredulous that she would want an average schmuck like me. "Nothing has changed, Nicki. I am still crazy for you!" I assured her. "I just hope that you won't change your mind about me after..." I was going to say "*after we get home to Seattle,*" but she reached out and pushed me back onto the bed.

"Silly man!" She laughed it as yanked open my bathrobe and crawled on top of me. "Not in a million years, not ever!" I could feel her wetness dripping down onto my cock as she bent over to kiss me passionately. The softness of her perky soft breasts mashed against my chest as she darted her tongue into my mouth felt wonderful. I reached both hands around her and gently grabbed her soft round bare ass. "Yesssss!" she purred softly.

I felt Nicki move her hand down between us and she carefully guided my rigid prick to the entrance of her drenched sex. The warmth of her slick wet pussy engulfing my dick was so very thrilling. "Yes, Nicki. Fuck me, baby. Fuck me!" I gasped. For the next several minutes, Nicki fucked me very slowly. In a squatting position, she would raise up till just my knob was still inside and then she would very slowly lower herself back down until I was completely buried inside. After about five minutes of this, my entire body was vibrating with the need to have all of her. I grabbed her hips and rolled her onto her back.

Nicki had a delightful grin on her face as I shoved a pillow under her ass and then lifted her legs back till her feet were next to her head. "Ooooh God yes!" she moaned loudly as I shoved my dick all the way into her dripping gaping hole "Fuck me. Fuck me, baby. Fuck me!" It was a very deep throaty moan. Smack, smack, smack, smack...I pounded into her so forcefully that she bounced against the bed as I drove into her over and over. "I am all yours!" I grunted as I thrusted into her again and again. The sensation of her sloppy wet sex was exquisite

Nicki had gotten me so aroused with her slow deliberate humping that I was ready to shoot off into her in just a few short moments. "Here it cums, baby. Here it cums!" My entire body tensed and then exploded in one long volcanic eruption. It was one very long gush that flooded my semen into her womb. My body was still vibrating as I felt her writhing beneath me when the sensation of my hot seed flowing into her caused her to climax too.

"That was fantastic!" Nicki moaned. The dreamy grin on her face conveyed the fact that she was satisfied. There was an absolute river of hot creamy cum oozing out of her when I pulled my dick out of her hole and rolled off of her.

"Wow!" I gasped in amazement. "Wow, baby!"

ALTHOUGH OUR morning frolic caused us to leave a little later than I had hoped that Sunday morning, we were able to make great progress that day since there was very little traffic on the road that day. Nicki was feeling exceptionally playful that day and sucked me off right there in the car as I cruised along at 70 MPH on the freeway. We pulled into Lincoln, Nebraska a couple of hours after dusk. We had a quick dinner in one of those nationwide restaurants and then found us a room.

Nicki and I took a long hot bath together and then made love. This time it was not the savage passionate rutting that we usually seem to enjoy so thoroughly. It was slow and tender and more intimate than anything I could ever remember. By the time we finished, I knew that I was lost to her forever. I could never do without her any more than I could do without air. "I could fall in love with you so easily!" I whispered it in her ear. Nicki giggled as she reached up and cupped my face in her hands.

"Don't be silly. We already are in love!" she told me softly. Then she kissed me very tenderly. I think I slept more soundly that night than I had ever experienced before.

She was sitting on the bed next to me when I woke up the next morning. She had already been up a while. She had showered, dressed and brought breakfast to me in bed. She looked sexy as hell in her shredded jeans. The sort that has about half dozen silts cut on the front of both legs right on top of the thighs. They have been washed enough to cause white frays in the cuts. I can clearly see her smooth tan thighs through the gaping holes.

"You really know how to make waking up a pleasure!" I teased her as I began to eat the egg and cheese muffin she had brought me. I almost bit my tongue when she got up to get the coffee she had left on the dresser. There were slits cut on the back of the jeans too. Right on top of her gorgeous ass cheeks. I got little glimpses of her terrific bare ass as she walked to the dresser. When she bent over to pick up the straw she had dropped, it became very obvious that she was not wearing any panties. "Oooh God, look at that!" I moaned.

"I thought you might like these!" she giggled as she brought me my coffee. My hands began to tremble as she removed her jacket. She was wearing a black transparent chiffon blouse that was very soft and very transparent. "Oh God, you are beautiful!" I gasped.

After I wolfed down my breakfast, I tried to pull her to me so I could strip her and ravage her gorgeous body. She slapped my hand and laughed as she informed me that I would have to wait until this evening. "I just want you to look at me and want me all day!" she informed me.

Although I was desperate to have her naked and take her relentlessly, it did amuse me that she had chosen to tantalise this way. Every time my cock got hard, I made it a point to pout about it so she would know it was working. I told her that it was slow cruel torture to make me suffer this way. Nicki just laughed at me and told me it was good for my character to learn some patience. I could clearly smell her musky scent. Proof that this was arousing her. That she was reveling in how deeply she excites me. "OK, baby. I'll wait!" I stuck out a pouty lip at her.

NICKI SLEPT most of the way across Wyoming. She looked so peaceful propped back with the back of her seat laid back. I had a perfect view of her lovely lily white tits through her transparent blouse. It took much self-restraint to not reach over and fondle her. By the time we were coming down Parley's Summit into Utah, I had made some plans for this evening in my mind. I had also figured out how to deal with the situation with Nicki's husband. It was just beginning to snow as we found a hotel in Ogden, Utah.

I told Nicki that I was too tired to go out to a restaurant for dinner. I suggested that we just call for a pizza delivery and then told her I needed to soak in the bathtub a while to relieve the stress and tightness of driving for ten hours. When she offered to join me, I told her I would rather just relax. I insinuated that I might be too tired for any sex play tonight. I had to bite my tongue when I saw the disappointment on her face. I could see that she was beginning to think that maybe it was a mistake to make me wait all day.

I had just dried off and put on some sweatpants and a sweatshirt when pizza boy arrived. I thought his eyes would bug out of his face when Nicki opened the door. His eyes were glued to her tits since he could see them through the fabric of her blouse. Then she dropped his money and I saw him shudder as she bent over to pick it up. He got a terrific view of her bare ass through the sliced back of her jeans. He groaned softly as she handed him the money and closed the door. "You made that poor guy cream himself!" I teased her. "Just like you tortured me all day!" I taunted.

I made it a point to eat my pizza very slowly. I even turned on the news and acted like I was waiting for the weather report. I even got Nicki to get my cola off the dresser, telling her my legs felt weak for all of the driving over the past three days. "I pushed myself too hard today!" I told her softly. Again she had that look of disappointment. I could see a bit of worry in her eyes. When we finished eating, I asked her if she would get the wet rag from the bathroom so I could wash the pizza oil off my face and hands. While she was gone, I turned off the TV and all the lights.

I was waiting for her as she came out of the bathroom. I grabbed her by the wrist and pulled her to the bed. She let out a little yelp as I threw her on the bed and ripped her blouse open. "I just can't wait another second!" I panted as I fondled her tits roughly. The shocked look on her face quickly turned to delight.

"Yes, take me, Aaron. Take all of me!" she gasped. After I undid the button on her jeans, I forced the zipper down and then yanked the crotch of her jeans until they ripped all the way to the back. Her sex was fully exposed to me as I pushed my sweatpants down to my knees.

"Take me, take me!" It was a loud guttural wailing sound as I slammed my dick straight into her quivering hole. I felt her fingernails digging into my ass in her attempt to pull me farther inside of her. "Take all of me, baby. Take all of me," she gasped. Each time that I thrust into her, I pressed in as far in as I could possibly go. Nicki was so aroused that her juices were oozing out. The scent of her sex aroused me even deeper. I was intoxicated with everything about this woman. Her beauty, her playfulness, her smell. I pounded into her relentlessly as her fingers tore at my flesh.

I savagely fucked Nicki like this for nearly twenty. I could feel the sting of her passion as my perspiration ran into the deep gouges that she has ripped into my ass cheeks and also on my back. "Give me your love, give it all to me!" she bellowed. I could feel her body thrashing back and forth as her orgasm started to overwhelm her. I shoved myself as far into her as I could reach and exploded into her belly.

"I love you, Nicki. I love you. I love you!" My body convulsed as I screamed out, as I flooded her with my seed, as I filled her with my love. "Oooh Geeeezus, Nicki. I love you!"

I absolutely slept like the dead that night. Nicki was spooned up against me with her yummy little ass pressed up against my belly. The stinging had subsided after she applied some healing ointment on the deep gouges.

I fell asleep deeply smitten with this soft, warm, beautiful woman who has captured every fiber of my being. And for the first time, it felt comfortable. For the very first time, I cherished it. I just floated away into bliss with her in my arms. I felt more wonderful inside than I could even begin to put into words.

Chapter Four

The drive from Utah to Seattle took us nearly 14 hours. But with the time difference between the two time zones, I had passed the marker in Oregon. It was just over 13 hours from the time we left till when we arrived at my condo in Downtown Seattle.

During the long trip, I told Nicki about my plan to deal with her husband. As long as she was OK with the possibility of losing her career, the straight forward approach would be the best bet.

RANDY LOOKED stunned as he was led away in handcuffs the next morning. It was especially satisfying that because it was the day before Thanksgiving, Randy would have to wait in jail till Monday for his arraignment hearing on Monday. Hank looked even more stunned as he was led away. They would both be facing charges of Blackmail, Extortion, Sex Slavery and Sex for Hire.

After viewing the videos and photographs, the police were confident that Randy had hung them both out to dry with the self-incriminating threats and remarks that had been recorded on the videos. After further investigation, the cops had proof that the video had come from Randy's cell phone and it had been sent from his home address. The cops said a first year law student could prosecute this case. They would both be facing a very long time in prison.

When we showed the video to Elisabeth, the CEO of the modelling agency, she sobbed and hugged Nicki tightly. "I'll see to it that neither one of them ever works in this town again!" She cried. After telling Nicki how deeply sorry she was that Nicki had been subjected to such sordid and depraved blackmail. Elisabeth assured Nicki that she could continue with the agency. Before we left, the photo shoot was rescheduled for after the New Year.

THERE WAS a knock on the door that Thanksgiving afternoon. When I opened the door, it was Amanda. She was by far the cutest little redhead that I had ever seen. I recognised her instantly from the videos I had seen of her at the police station. Most of them were of her having sex with Nicki since she was Randy's newest target and had not manipulated her to fuck other men yet. I could feel a wiggle in my jeans as I remembered how sexy she is naked.

I was surprised when she threw herself into my arms and kissed me vigorously. "I just want to thank you for what you did!" It came out all broken up in between the kisses. I glanced over and saw Nicki smiling at us. I felt a pang of worry that she might feel jealous about Amanda hanging all over me. I noticed that it was a devilish sort of grin as Amanda finally pulled away from me. My cock was erect and bulging in my jeans.

Nicki informed me while we were finished making preparations for our Thanksgiving meal that she had invited Amanda to join us for dinner. "She was so excited to come over and thank you personally for all you've done for us!" Nicki told me. Then, she informed me that Amanda had a very special surprise for me. When I tried to press her further for more details, she banished me from the kitchen. She suggested that I go "freshen up" for later. "Just let us girls finish the kitchen work in peace!" She scolded.

When I came back downstairs an hour later, it seemed very quiet in the house. I thought that I heard some muffled giggles from the kitchen so I quietly peeked around the corner when I got to the entrance. I was amazed as I glanced to the back of the room and saw them together. They were locked in a very passionate French kiss. Amanda had her left hand down the back of Nicki's pants and was squeezing on her ass cheeks. Nicki had her right hand up the front of

Amanda's top and was fondling her tits. My dick was fully rigid as I very quietly went back out to the living room.

I turned on the TV and pretended to be interested in the football game as they started to bring out the food to the dining room. I was hoping my cock would go soft before I had to get up to go to the table. But my mind kept seeing them locked together kissing and touching each other. When they called me to the table, I pulled out my shirt tail to cover the throbbing bulge in my jeans.

With them seated side by side, it was impossible to erase that memory of them. "Did you enjoy the show?" Nicki broke the silence. She must have seen the confused look on my face as she asked it. "The football game!" she giggled playfully.

"We were so busy we never heard you come downstairs," Amanda added. I noticed that they looked up at each other and sort of smiled innocently.

"It sure got hot in there!" Nicki winked at Amanda as she said it. I saw a flush come to Amanda's face as they both giggled.

As soon as dinner was over, they told me to go upstairs and wait for them. Nicki suggested that I get "more comfortable." She suggested that I put on some sweatpants. I heard some more soft giggling downstairs as I was getting changed. The only clue that they gave me was that it was going to be the most terrific surprise in my life.

Twenty minutes later, I heard them coming up the stairs. When they came into the room, Nicki came over to the side of the bed and bent over to kiss me on the cheek. "You trust me, don't you?" She whispered it in my ear. When I told her yes, she informed me that she was going to blindfold me and restrain my arms and legs. She insisted that it was all necessary for my surprise.

I must say that I felt a little apprehensive as Nicki carefully blindfolded me and tethered me to the bedposts. With all the things these two girls have been subjected to at the hands of greedy lustful men, I began to worry that they might take out their tortured pain on me. My fears became complete alarm when they started to cut my sweatpants off with a sharp pair of scissors. They also cut off my tank top. I was now tied up, spread eagle and completely naked.

I then heard whispering and rustling around the room. I felt someone get onto the bed near my feet followed by another pressure as the other got on the bed next to my head. *"This is it...they are going to kill me now!"* I thought to myself. For a moment, I heard the sounds of kissing. Then I felt more movement.

I suddenly felt the exquisite sensation of a hot wet mouth engulfing my soft prick. "Oooh God!" I gasped softly. I heard a giggle right next to me and then felt the soft warmth of a breast being pressed against my lips. My dick began to swell rapidly as I now realised that they were both doing me together. There was no way I could tell which one was sucking my cock or which one had a tit in my mouth. It was glorious! I don't know how long this lasted, but it was absolutely the most deliciously erotic experience I had ever had.

Then, without warning, they stopped. I heard them leave the room and then heard some whispering in the hallway. I felt the pressure on the bed as they both climbed back next to me. There was a momentary silence but I again heard sounds of kissing and soft moans. I felt one of them move on top of me over my belly and a soft warm hand grasped my throbbing prick.

My entire body vibrated as I felt her hot dripping pussy sliding all the way down my cock till I was buried to the root. I heard a soft moan as her body quivered and her fluid oozed out onto my thighs. Then I felt a movement over my face and felt some drips of fluid falling onto my chin. And then her pussy was grinding into my mouth. I knew instantly from the taste of her sweet pussy that it was Nicki that was riding my face and it was Amanda that was fucking me!

"Oooh, Nicki. You were right, he's delicious!" It was Amanda that finally spoke first. She was rocking back and forth slowly on my prick and I could feel her hands pressed against my belly.

"Please, baby, let me see you. Let me see you," I begged Nicki softly. I felt her raise up just enough to reach between her legs to yank down the blindfold.

I was ecstatic when I saw Amanda impaled on my cock. She was tossing her head back and forth as she humped me. She had the most wonderful look of bliss on her face.

"Eat me, baby. Eeeeeeat me!" Nicki moaned as I shoved my tongue up into her drenched hole. It thrilled me to see them kissing and fondling each other as they humped me together.

I had never dreamed that an average guy like me would ever get to experience a threesome like this with two such beautiful young women. Never in a million years would I have believed that I would be here with these two gorgeous models. I could never have even fantasized how truly marvelous this reality would be.

As I felt the load building up for the release, I sucked really hard on Nicki's clit. Just as she began to climax on my face, my cock erupted deep into Amanda's vagina. I could feel Amanda beginning to convulse into her orgasm as she felt the heat of my semen flooding into her.

"Oooh my God...Yesssss!" she moaned loudly. Nicki bent forward and they kissed passionately. I shot off one last time. After they untied me, we all fell to sleep all entwined together. It felt wonderful to drift off sandwiched between them.

THEY WERE in the shower together when I woke up in the morning. A couple of minutes after the water shut off, Amanda came into the room. When she got to the side of the bed, she dropped her towel to the floor, pulled back the blankets.

"Nicki told me to say good morning," she whispered as she climbed on top of me and mounted my prick.

She was already rocking back and forth on my rigidness when Nicki came to the bed completely naked.

"Can Amanda come live with us, pleeeeeeeeze?" She whispered it as she pressed a tit into my mouth. How could I possibly say no?

THE END

Here is a sample from another story you may enjoy:

Jack Ryder

In Love
WITH A
COUGAR
Erotic Romance

I STARTED dating Veronica during the summer after her senior year in high school. We had met at a graduation party. She was a neighbor of my friend Bobby that was throwing the after commencement gala. It was a fairly tame party since his parents and several other parents were there to chaperone the goings on.

I was quite smitten with Veronica from the very start. She told me much later that she had felt the same way, but that night, she was quite aloof and played hard to get. By the time I walked her home at midnight, she loosened up a little. She kissed me on the cheek and handed me a small slip of paper with her cell phone number on it. "I'd be OK with seeing you again." She said it very softly as she kissed my cheek a second time.

Although Veronica's dad was not real pleased, her mother Gynn was very cordial and seemed to enjoy watching me and Veronica fawn all over one another from the very start. The problem with her father's mistrust seemed to be a suspiciousness based on his own misdeeds. For one, he had knocked up Gynn on their graduation night thus leading to their marriage. The second misdeed came to the surface two months later when he dumped Gynn for his 20-year-old office assistant.

The next couple of months were difficult for Veronica as she tried her best to sooth her mother's hurt and emptiness. Rather than going out on dates, I spent a lot of time with the both of them just hanging out. Helping out with the "manly chores." It was a simple thing to do and it just felt right to lend a hand in any way that I could.

By Christmas time, Veronica and I had progressed to the point that we often petted one another as we watched TV alone in the den. Veronica had very perky 34C breasts that were slightly upturned. I adored how her nipples would become erect whenever I slipped my hand up her top and fondled them. There were several times that I managed to give her an orgasm just by playing with her tits.

There were times that Gynn nearly caught us. She would suddenly be in the hall wanting to know if we wanted popcorn or ice cream or any of various other types of snacks. It sometimes seemed like she had a sixth sense as to when I was just about to get into Veronica's pants. It seemed like every time I had her just at the point that she would allow me to go further, Gynn would arrive all happy and giggly.

It was the first week in spring when I finally managed to get my hand down inside Veronica's pants. I was ecstatic when I found that her panties were soaking wet as I rubbed my finger up and down the sloppy crease in her panties. Veronica had just begun to rub up and down on the bulge in my jeans when I heard Gynn coming up the hall. I felt Veronica shudder as I pulled my hand out of her pants. She later told me that I had got her off that night. I was very frustrated when I got home that night.

When I got into bed that night, I could still smell her on my fingers. My dick got really hard as I remembered how wet her pussy had been. As I began to stroke my cock, I remembered how her body had trembled as I fingered her gash. I remembered how her breathing had changed and how she had softly moaned in a soft whisper.

I remembered Gynn coming in the door after I pulled my hand out of Veronica's pants and how she was smiling at me. Then I remembered the quick glimpse I got of Gynn as I was leaving the house. Her blinds were open in her room and for a brief moment, I had seen her topless. My dick erupted as I remembered how lovely her 36C cone shaped tits had looked.

It was that same night that I had learned that her mother was really a step-mother. I had never really thought about it much since they are both Latina women. Both with the dark olive brown smooth skin. Both with long silky coal black hair and eyes that look like little black opals. It had never occurred to me that they did not resemble each other that much.

Veronica is a very petite 5 foot 2 and Gynn is 5 foot 9 and a very voluptuous 36C-28-36. It had flabbergasted me when Veronica had told me that Gynn was only 32 years old. When her dad had dumped Gynn, she had chosen to live with Gynn because they had been together for 12 years and Veronica thought it would be weird to live with her 40-year old Dad and his 20-year old pregnant mistress.

Most of this was all so very new to me that I had no way to process everything that was going on at the time. I had just turned 19 the week before school had started and Veronica had turned 18 just a couple of weeks after me.

Although she had boyfriends before me, she was my very first. She was the only girl I had ever touched in a sexual way. She had been the only one to allow me to peek at her tits. She had been the first girl, not in a magazine, that I had ever fantasized about. Until tonight! It had been Gynn that I was thinking about when I sprayed my jizz all over my stomach tonight. It was Gynn that I was thinking about as I fell off to sleep.

It was early May when I found out that I was in danger of flunking out of my college Algebra class at the local Junior college. Veronica offered to have me come over so she could tutor me in the evenings for the rest of the quarter. Hopefully that would raise my grade enough to pass the class.

Over the next five weeks, I spent almost every night at their house. When I wasn't doing the algebra, I did my other homework assignments. I was pretty much there every evening from 6 p.m. till midnight. On the weekends, I did the "manly chores" like washing and waxing cars, mowing the lawn, cleaning leaves from the rooftop gutters. All the stuff a "man around the house" would normally do.

I remember the first time I heard that term. I had just finished cleaning out the garage for Gynn and she had brought me a glass of lemonade. "It's nice having a man around the house to do all this messy stuff!" She had said it softly. It had made me swell with pride that she had referred to me as a man! She was the first to ever call me that.

I could tell by the way her breasts were pressed against her tight cotton t-shirt that she was not wearing a bra. It was the first time that I remember thinking that I wished that she was my girlfriend instead of Veronica. I had to quickly glance away when it seemed like she saw me staring at her tits.

If you enjoyed this sample then look for **In Love with a Cougar**.

Also by this Author

The Handyman Seduction

The Beer Bust Scandal

Scandalous Emotion

Intimate Relation

The Seduction of Kimi

Erotic Goes Hi-Tech

One at a Time

The Wizard Casey's Coven

The Inn Keeper's Wizard: When Love and Magic
Collide

Trailer Trash Payback

Queer Intentions

Zoe's Fun House

Public Display

Test Drive

About the Author

Jack Ryder LOVES everything there is about sex!

When he is not involved with his "swinger" friends, enjoying a steamy threesome, or being part of a raunchy "gang bang", you can find him on first class planes, trains, and cruise ships. Traveling seems to be the BEST way to finding new and interesting sexmates for him. Sexmates. Plural. He lives with the saying "The More, The Merrier!"

He owns a successful business in New York. He writes as a hobby and also as sort of documentation of his mind-blowing sexcapades over the years. He is presently roaming around the streets of Manhattan but can be anywhere in the world too, since he travels often. So, beware! You just might be his next mate.

*"The most fun thing I enjoy when writing my stories is trying to figure out which is fantasy and which was memory. ENJOY! (Preferably with a friend. *wink*) " -Jack Ryder-*

From the Author

If you have any comments, suggestions, or would just like to get a little personal, please feel free to email me at:
jack_ryder@awesomeauthors.org

If you enjoyed any of my books then please share the love and click like on my books in Amazon.

If you write me a review and send me an email I will send you a free book, or many.
(Just know that these emails are filtered by my publisher.)

Good news is always welcome.

One Last Thing, For Kindle Readers...

When you turn the page, Kindle will give you the opportunity to rate this book and share your thoughts on Facebook and Twitter. If you enjoyed my writings, would you please take a few seconds to let your friends know about it? Because... when they enjoy they will be grateful to you and so will I.

Thank You!

Jack Ryder
jack_ryder@awesomeauthors.org